Fly Away, Little Birdie

by
Stacy Doley
illustrations by
Lacrymosa

ISBN 978-0-9985699-2-5

Printed in the U.S.A.
First printing. June 2018
Edited by Critique Editing Services, LLC

To Naomi, my greatest blessing

Grandpa Jake held his grandson's trembling hand as they sat inside the car. "It's gonna be alright, son. You'll see," said Grandpa Jake. "You're gonna have a really good day today." Coby was too nervous and too afraid to speak. He looked anxiously out the car window at the big red, brick building that loomed before his eyes.

"C'mon." Grandpa Jake moved toward the driver side car door in order to step out of the vehicle.

"Wait!" Coby's voice rose with anxiety. "Maybe we can come back later, Grandpa."

"But we've already circled the block ten times." Grandpa Jake looked at his grandson with warm and understanding eyes.

"Just one more time around, Grandpa. I'll be ready then." Coby squeezed Grandpa Jake's hand as tight as his five-year-old fingers would allow him to.

Grandpa Jake sighed softly to himself. This was the fourth child he'd had the joy of bringing to school on their very first day. Aniyah, Maurice and Kenya were all happy to go to school, but it was a very different story with little Coby. When Grandpa Jake and Grandma Minnie told Coby he would be going to school, he hid under the covers of his bed and refused to come out. Grandma Minnie was able to coax him out with some milk and sugar cookies.

The cookies were now in a small brown paper bag that rested on Coby's leg. Coby pulled out one cookie and took a small bite as his grandfather started the engine and began to drive one more time around the block.

Grandpa smiled as he turned the steering wheel. "You know, Coby, I've been where you are," he said, "although it was a long time ago. It's natural to be afraid of things you've never been through before. But let me tell you a story that my father told me that helped me get through my first day of school. It's about a little robin named Little Birdie."

Once upon a time there was a young robin named Little Birdie. Little Birdie was one of a brood of four, and he was the youngest. He loved the comfort of the nest and his mother's warm feathers. He was almost three weeks old, and he was excited because his mother said she wanted to talk to Little Birdie and his brother and sisters.

Mother Robin stood, at the top of the nest and spoke to her little ones. "Today, my young robins, is the day you learn how to fly!" And with that Mother Robin flapped her wings and flew a few feet from the nest to a nearby tree, and then she quickly flew back and regained her footing at the top of the nest.

"I'm so proud of all of you and how you have grown up to be such good, strong birds. Now it's time for you to leave the nest and start your own families." Mother Robin beamed at her birds as she spoke from the crest of her nest.

"Watch me, little ones," Mother Robin spoke in a calm, yet jubilant tone as she demonstrated the art of flying while her brood watched. Little Birdie looked with his beak half open and his eyes wide as his mother soared high above the nest.

"See how easy it is?" Mother Robin demonstrated the technique of flying many, many times.

Little Birdie felt dizzy watching his mother fly around so much. He worried that he wasn't going to be able to fly like his mother.

What if I fall? Little Birdie wondered. He peeked out of the nest and onto the ground. *That's a long way down*, he said to himself.

In his heart Little Birdie really didn't want to leave the nest. *I don't know what's out there in that world outside my home*, Little Birdie thought. *What if the other birds are mean to me? What if I don't find a family?* Little Birdie had all kinds of questions that made him feel even more afraid to fly.

Little Birdie began to tremble with fear. He thought about how he could get out of flying and leaving the nest. Maybe he could tell his mother his wing was broken and he would have to wait until it healed before he could fly. Or maybe he could say he was too weak to fly. After all, it was almost noon and he hadn't had lunch yet.

"Okay, my sweet birds," Mother Robin said. "Now you try. I know you can do it!"

Little Birdie looked around at his brother and sisters, hoping he wasn't the only one who was afraid to fly.

Little Birdie watched with disappointment as each of his siblings imitated their mother. One by one they perched themselves on top of the nest and flew out of it. "See ya, wouldn't want to be ya," said his oldest sister. She flapped her wings feverishly and flew with great effort to a nearby branch on the next tree.

"Adios, amigos!" shouted Little Birdie's brother who seemed to glide out of the nest and onto a lower branch on the same tree. "Wow! This is so much fun!"

"I'm free! I'm free!" Little Birdie heard his other sister squawk as she tumbled out of the nest. "Wh- wh-whoa!" she stammered, almost tripping over a tree branch in an effort to land.

Little Birdie gasped. *Oh, my goodness*, he thought. *She almost fell.* Little Birdie ran up to his mother and hid under her wing. "My sister almost fell, Mother. Did you see that? Oh, I don't think I can do it! I don't think I wanna do it! Flying is not for me. Don't make me go out there. I don't think I was meant to fly." The words poured out of Little Birdie like a bucket of rainwater.

"Oh, honey, you weren't just meant to fly," Mother Robin said as she hugged Little Birdie tightly, "you, my dear robin, were *born* to fly!"

And with that, Mother Robin flapped her wings and soared high above the nest and came back and landed right in front of Little Birdie. "You'll never know what you can do until you try, son."

"Just look at your brother and sisters," Mother Robin remarked. "If they can do it, you can do it, too."

Little Birdie shook his head. "But they're older than I am, Mother. It's different for them."

"Oh, nonsense," Mother Robin said with a hint of frustration. "Little Birdie, you were born to fly, now get out there and fly." And with that, Mother Robin gently pushed Little Birdie out of the nest.

Little Birdie grabbed hold of a part of the nest. "Help!" he shrieked. "Mother, save me, please!"

"Just let go," Mother Robin said to Little Birdie. "Let go, and flap your wings. Fly away, Little Birdie. You can do it. Fly away."

"But I'm afraid, Mother. I just can't. Please, help me."

Feeling a deep sense of compassion for her child, Mother Robin pulled Little Birdie back into the nest. While clutching his chest, Little Birdie nestled himself in his mother's feathers. "Whew! For a minute there I thought I was a goner," cried Little Birdie.

Immediately Mother Robin knew what she had to do.

Mother Robin wrapped a comforting wing around Little Birdie and she began to tell him why he could fly. "Little Birdie, I know you can fly," Mother Robin said, "because you're my special, little bird." Mother Robin's eyes twinkled.

"I was so happy on the day you were hatched because I saw that you were special. I knew you were smart and you were going to grow up to be one of the strongest birds in the nest. I remember when you were hatched, you broke the shell with your egg tooth and pushed your way out of that shell in record time. When you opened your mouth, you opened your mouth wider than any of my other fledglings."

"Really?" Little Birdie asked.

"Really, my birdie. And you've grown up to be so strong and healthy. Your feathers are so beautiful. You remind me of your father, because his feathers were just that beautiful. He would soar high, almost into the clouds because he was proud of what he looked like."

"I remind you of Dad?" Little Birdie asked in astonishment. Little Birdie began to beam with pride as he remembered the times he saw his father flying to the nest to help his mother care for the clutch. Little Birdie felt very special because he never heard her say these things about his brother and sisters.

After their conversation, Mother Robin asked Little Birdie if he would try to fly. "I know you can do it," Mother Robin said. "You have the feathers for it." She winked at Little Birdie as she spoke to him.

Little Birdie smiled at his mother and decided he would give flying a try after all. With his legs quivering and his stomach seemingly in knots, Little Birdie walked to the top of the nest. He saw his brother and sisters watching him. His mother stood behind him and smiled lovingly with her eyes.

It's now or never, Little Birdie thought to himself. But somehow he knew he could do it.

Little Birdie took a deep breath, pushed off with his feet and began flapping his wings in the air. Little Birdie flew all around. He flew above the nest and landed gracefully on the branch of a nearby tree. He looked at his brother and sisters perched on different tree branches. One by one, Little Birdie watched each of them fly away. Without fear or trepidation, Little Birdie puffed his chest out, pushed off with his feet and flew away.

Mother Robin watched with pride as Little Birdie soared through the air. Then she sighed softly within herself, smiled with her eyes and flew away.

Grandpa Jake pulled up to the front of the school building and turned off the car engine. He turned toward Coby and smiled. "You know, Coby, just like Little Birdie, you remind me of your dad on his first day of school. He was scared, too, and he really didn't want to go to school on that first day. But you know what he told me after it was all over?"

Coby looked at his grandfather with curiosity in his eyes.

"He told me how much he enjoyed his first day of school because everybody was so nice to him. He made some really good friends and one day he told me how much he loved going to school."

"You remind me so much of him," Grandpa Jake continued. "You're strong like he was at your age. Smart and handsome, too." Grandpa Jake smiled wide, revealing one missing tooth on the side of his mouth.

Coby smiled with him, revealing a few of his own missing teeth. Coby didn't realize that he was just like his father. He respected and admired his father because he was a soldier in the military. Coby knew his dad had to spend a lot of time away from home because he was doing brave things overseas to help his country. Coby's heart lifted as he thought of being like his father.

With trembling hands and a mouth full of cotton, Coby opened the car door and stepped out. Grandpa Jake got out on the other side and walked over to Coby. Coby grabbed his grandpa's hand and clutched his bag of cookies in the other hand. Coby gained confidence with each step he took as he walked toward the school. He was ready to fly.

Comprehension Questions

Directions: Answer each question using text evidence.

1. What is the setting of each story?

2. Are the settings important to the stories?

3. Is Coby part of a traditional family?

4. What message is the author trying to share?

5. Is this a realistic story?

www.ingramcontent.com/pod-product-compliance
Lightning Source LLC
Chambersburg PA
CBHW041005170626
46815CB00002B/175